THE LOST RELIGION

BY

LEVI TAYLOR

*To Mrs. Phillips
I hope you enjoy
the book.
Levi Taylor*

Levi Taylor

Published by Mrs. Bea's Kids Publishing
Copyright 2010

All rights reserved. No parts of this book may be reproduced, stored in or reproduced into a retrieval system, or transmitted, in any form by any means (electronic, mechanical, photocopying, recording, or otherwise) without prior written consent from the publisher.

This is a work of fiction.

First print April 2010
Printed in the United States of America

Cover copyright©2010 by **Mrs. Bea's Publishing**

All rights reserved and applicable under all Federal Copyright Laws

Cover Illustration: Lynn Morgan
Editor: Sharee P. Miller

ISBN: 978-0-9825821-3-8

DEDICATION

To my Lord God and my Savior Jesus.

Levi Taylor

ACKNOWLEDGEMENTS

I would like to thank my Lord God for granting me this gift. And for helping me see that I was meant to write for him. Also I am thanking him for helping me find my place in this big world. Thank you God!

I would like to thank my deceased mother for raising me, and everything she has done for me. I know you are no longer with us, but I love you and miss you dearly, thank you for everything mom!

I would like to thank my illustrator Lynn Morgan, for doing the book cover. It is beautiful. I love it. Thank you!

I would like to thank my friends at school for encouraging me. I couldn't figure out what to do for the story or where to begin. My friends were there for me encouraging me. Thank you all my wonderful friends. You are all awesome!

I would like to thank my publisher Terri Williams. If she hadn't helped me out, my dream of being an author would not be happening so early in my life. It still shocks me even now. I want to cry. Thank you Terri!!!!!!

I would like to thank my family. They have been there for me, and through this with me. They were there and still are they're encouraging me on. But there is a certain person in my family I would like to thank in person. Thanks Family!

And the certain family member I would like to thank is my grandmother. Grandma, we have our differences but that does not keep me from loving you. Thank you for encouraging me to keep writing. Thank you for taking care of me. And thank you for being there for me when I needed help or comfort or anything. You are the best and second best mother I could ever have. That's why you are the best grandmother and second mother I could ever have. Thank you so much for everything you have done for me. I love you. Thank you!

Prologue

There was a time when all lands were filled with peace and quiet. The birds once sang their song, and the trees danced with the wind. A time when rivers were clean, and the skies a beautiful shade of blue; the ground full of greenery and the air warm.

A time when everyone worshiped one and only one God. The only God that created this world; the creator. Everyone everywhere was worshiping this Glorious God. This religion became known as Christianity.

Then God's people began doing things God didn't want them doing. They were considered to be sinning. The more these people sinned, the further away they got from God. But the closer they got to Satan, one of God's fallen angels. Then Satan found ways to reform these people into doing his bidding.

One of these people, Satan gave power to. When Satan gave the man power, it changed the man's appearance and thoughts about the world, about everything. This man was then known to everyone as the most terrifying living being to live. They gave him the name Dark Lord.

That wasn't the end of Satan's doing. From there came the blood-lusting creatures of the night called Vampires. There were enormous reptiles with huge scaly bat-like wings that breathed fire. They became known to everyone as Dragons. The dragons roamed the skies. There also came other disgusting creatures all from the dark side to do Satan's bidding.

When this happened, God created elves that looked like humans, but they had pointy ears, flawless skin, long beautiful hair, and were all tall. There were immortals. Some immortals looked exactly like humans, while others took on different forms.

Then along came the Avain's, second to rule the skies. Avain's looked like humans, all but for the wings and turning into over size birds. God gave the elves power, and some immortals power. He then sent them to fight the Dark.

And thus began The First Great War. The land's peace and quiet was disturbed and replaced with destruction and the sound of metal colliding. All critters of the forest hid; no sound or song came from them. Trees fell against their will while the wind howls monstrous. Rivers soon became stained with blood, and the skies now pitch black, all while the air became cold as a winter night.

Over the centuries, the battle between good and evil went on, back and forth. There was no telling who had the upper hand. One minute, the Dark side was in the lead, and then another minute, the Light side was in the lead.

Then came one of the worst days in history. The Dark Lord used his power on nine innocent living beings and gave them power. This power did the same thing it did to him. It changed their appearance and thoughts. This power allowed these nine living beings to transform into any form they desired and gave them more power to do what they wish with it. They became known as the Dark Lord's Deadly Nine Shape shifters.

Along with the Shape shifters came the Assassins. There are ten assassins. They all dressed alike, but they can tell you a different story looking into their eyes. The ten Assassins do all the dirty work that goes on behind the scenes for the Dark Lord. When this happened, the Dark side gained the upper hand.

When all hope could be lost, God created the seven crystals. The first being blue, represents water. The second being green, representing earth. The third is red, for the burning flames of a fire. The fourth was clear, for the air all around us. The fifth was a golden yellow, for life. And the sixth was black, for death.

When all six were gathered, it created the seventh crystal, which were many colors. When in the right hands, could be used for good. When in the wrong hands, disasters there will be.

The Lost Religion

Few of God's followers were chosen to be the crystals keepers. They used the crystal in the war and gained the upper hand for quite awhile. Just as everyone thought the Good side was winning, someone betrayed them.

The keepers destroyed the crystal and hid the six crystals in places no one would dare look. The war was soon coming to an end anyway. God's people found other ways to fight the Dark side. And when the war was over, everything went back to normal.

The trees grew back and once more danced with the wind. The birds came out and sung their song. Rivers no longer were stained with blood. The sky, back to its beautiful shade of blue. And the air warms with the lands full of greenery once more.

Eventually, the people of God strayed away and began worshiping other things. Bibles were destroyed everywhere.

People began to think Bibles and Christianity was the doing of the Dark Lord. When the Bibles were destroyed, an elf hid one with magic so only the chosen one may be able to read it in the future.

This elf was the only one who still worshiped God and believed in Christianity. She fell ill one day and wasn't getting better. She became the last person to remember Christianity. Over time, the elf women wrote a prophecy before she passed away. When she passed away, so did Christianity. From there on Christianity became known as The Lost Religion.

Everyone knew this prophecy, but only the elves believed in it.

What it says is this:

'There will be a day when The Dark Lord and his minions will come again. This time they will be much stronger and more terrifying than before.

Then all the lands will be disturbed once more. The skies will be pitch black filled with thunder and lightning. All the water will be stained with so much blood, that it will turn black and violent.

The only way to fight the Dark this time is to fight with the Chosen Warrior of Light. The warrior will come and bring back The Lost Religion. The Lost Religion will spread throughout the lands slowly at first. But it will come to everyone. When The Lost Religion has been restored, and the warrior has found the other chosen ones, then there will be war once more.

This will not be any war. This will be the worst war of all wars; The Second Great War. It will be worse than the First Great War in many ways. This War will decide the fate of the world. And the weight of the world will be on the shoulder of the Chosen Warrior of the Light.

Will the Dark Lord control the world for eternity? Or will the Warrior and chosen ones be able to save the world from the Dark Lord and restore peace forever.

It may be years or thousands of years before any of this happens. No matter how long it takes, this will happen.'

Once everything was restored and peace came once more. Everyone could sleep at night knowing no one would hurt them ever again. And all the critters of the forest also came out.

Every living thing went on with their life pretending that the First Great War never happened. No one was worried about the Dark rising.

Even as the elf that wrote the prophecy and passed away, somewhere in a dark place, the very first shape shifters were alive and stirring trouble even as you read this.

So mark my words, the Dark Lord is coming and it may be sooner than you think.

Chapter One
Ena

Strolling through the lush green forest, you can smell the morning dew. The birds singing their morning song. The sun shines brightly warming everything up. Forest critters just waking up from a long night slumber.

I walk beside my brown stallion on the old worn out path from horses and wagons coming and going. About a few hours of walking, I finally stumble upon what looks like a very small village. No, it's not a small village. More like a training ground camp thing.

I watch as a group of teenager's swordplay. I love watching groups of newbie's learn how to sword play. It is so fascinating. When you didn't block correctly, you would always collect bruises, but for some reason newbie's have no patience.

Levi Taylor

I sit on the low stonewall and watch the teenagers. While watching, I decide to take my hair down and put it back up in a nicer ponytail. Then I braid my maroon hair.

I could hear the man with long hair yelling at the newbie's. Then the newbie's get back up and keep trying. It's so funny. They think they know everything, but when you get them to show you what they know, they don't know hardly anything at all.

When they started putting stuff away, I could tell they were done for the day. So, I jumped off the stone wall. Then got ready to start out into the forest until I heard footsteps behind me. I turn around on my heels to find the man from earlier. I looked up to him. Wow, this man had to be at least six feet. Amazing. And he looked to be in his early thirties.

He asks me, "What can I do for a beautiful girl like you Miss?"

Was he flirting with me? That is so disgusting! "I thought

this was a village, but apparently I was wrong. If you don't mind, I'll be on my way then."

The man then asks me, "What is it you need? If it's food, I can get that for you Miss."

This makes no sense what so ever. First this stranger flirts with me, now he's offering me food. Make up your mind Sir! "I am not in need of food Sir. I have been traveling in search of work that will pay me well. So far I have not found any place. And I am guessing this place is in no need of any more help. So, good day Sir."

I go to leave, but this man is stubborn enough to get in my way. At this point I was starting to get mad. "You are wrong Miss. Yes this place looks like it needs no help, but that is where you are wrong. This place is in need of a lot of help. Maybe if we go see Mistress Raven, she will hire you to work here. How does that sound?"

Ok, that did sound like a very good offer, so how could I

say no. But who in the world is this Mistress Raven lady. "That sounds really good, but who is this Mistress Raven? I have never heard of a Mistress Raven."

The man just laughs, "A northerner who has never heard of Mistress Raven. That is quite unique. Mistress Raven is a northerner who bought this place to train people for the king's army. So in other words, she is in charge of this place. Come along Miss…"

He takes my horse's reins and heads in the opposite direction that I don't want to go in, "Where are my manners? I am Seth. I do almost all the cooking for the trainees. As you seen before, I also help with the weapons training. You can usually find me out here or in the mess hall's kitchen cooking. So what is your name Miss?"

Finally I follow Seth, "My name is Ena sir."

Seth began talking about something that had to do with cooking, which I had no clue about. We walk over a well built stone bridge, past a big orchard and what looks like maybe the bathhouse on the other side of the road, and up to a huge building. Seth ties my horse up, and leads me inside the beautiful detail double door of the building.

We were in a big hall way with a spiral staircase on the left, and quite a bit of classrooms maybe. I follow Seth to the end of the hallway where I wait outside while he goes into a room with smaller double doors than the entrance doors, but still with such detail. To my left, I see a door open and get a glimpse of books. Maybe there's a library here too.

Seth comes back out and gets me. I follow him inside the room. It was small but still a really nice size room. There was a lady at least in her late twenties to early thirties. Really hard to tell. She has black hair like coal in the tightest bun I have ever seen. And she was wearing nothing but black robes. The robes that look like dresses, almost.

Levi Taylor

This lady was sitting behind a messy desk where papers and books were piled high and scattered everywhere. Looking around, I notice a door that probably leads to another room. There was a single big arch window with a built in bench and the walls were filled with more books.

A tired steady voice says, "You are Ena? I am Mistress Raven, the lady in charge here. Tell me your full name and where you came from."

So, I introduce myself, "My full name is Lady Ena Scanrall, youngest child in my family. I come from a beautiful city that is far north called Sira."

Mistress Raven reminds me of a black raven. Anyway, the Black Raven gets up and moves with such grace, you'd think she was a queen. She gracefully walks toward me. And her shoes did not make a noise.

She stops in front of me and says, "You will tell me about yourself. How old you are? Why is a noble like you so far from home? And you will tell me about your history. Then I may consider if you will stay or not."

I look the Black Raven in the eyes, "If you are trying to scare me, it is not working. Even if you are not going to hire me, I will tell you about myself. There are three children in my family. The oldest is my sister Myra, the middle is my brother Bruce, and then comes me. A bandit killed my brother when I was only ten. And I am now one hundred and fifty years old, but I like to look sixteen. Anyway, when Bruce was killed, I picked up swordplay and learned how to use other weapons. Of course my parents did not approve of it. Eventually my father, Lord Scanrall took me under his wing and taught me everything he could teach me about weapons and how to use them. He taught me that all before my mother sent me to a school for magicians. I enjoy learning new things. I am a nature person; so if you or anyone ever needs me, check the woods. And that is my story Mistress Raven."

The black Raven picks up some books and begins putting them back on their shelf. "What do you expect to gain here?" asks the Black Raven, "I cannot baby you like you are used to. You will work just as hard as everyone else without using magic to finish quickly. You will be paid the same amount as everyone. And you will not be getting any special treatments."

"I expect to gain experience. Experience I could not gain in the north. I expect to be treated exactly like everyone else or you will be hearing complaints from me. And I understand the terms for working here clearly. I will obey them."

'I can't believe this girl. She is not fooling around. I suppose I can hire her, but I'll send for a friend of mine to keep an eye on her.' Thinks Raven.

"How well do you work around animals?" asks the Black Raven.

The Lost Religion

This was quite surprising, "What? I'm sorry. The question caught me off guard. To answer your question, I never really learned how to tend to animals, but I am willing to learn."

The Black Raven turns to the chef who was sitting in a chair reading near the double door, and she says, "If you are not too busy Seth, I have things I need you to do."

Seth closes his book and stands, "I am not too busy Mistress."

The Black Raven returns back to her desk, "Take her to Martha and tell Martha to get Ena some used clothes and some nice clothes. Then leave Ena with Martha. You are then to find Nasir. Tell Nasir to have a room prepared for Ena. Also tell him, that she will be helping him and his son in the stable and the barn with the animals. After that, return to me. I have other errands for you to run for me."

Seth nods his head, and looks at me, "Come along now Miss."

Levi Taylor

I bow respectfully to the Black Raven and follow Seth through the hallways again. This time a few of the classrooms were full with an adult or two teaching. Once outside, we go straight to a building that was pretty small. Inside, Seth leaves me in the front and goes into another room yelling something.

When he returns, a woman was behind him. "This lady here is Martha, the seamstress here. She designs and makes most of the clothes for us."

The woman was at least in her mid fifties. Her hair was curly like a spring and a sunflower golden color blond that goes to her shoulders. Her eyes were as blue as the sky, but told a story behind them. She asks me, "Are you Ena Scanrall that Seth here is talking about?"

I slightly bow, "Yes ma'am."

"I guess I'll be seeing you later then." Say's Seth. The redhead leaves closing the door behind him.

Martha has me follow her into another room full of clothes. She begins rummaging through some clothes, "Ena dear, what colors do you like? Better yet, what colors do you usually wear?"

"I wear a lot of earth tone colors, mostly different shades of greens like the leaves on a tree or the vines on a plant in the summer. I then wear light or dark browns with greens. I also wear dark blues with grays and blacks."

The kind lady finds me some shirts and pants in the colors I like to wear. She gives them to me and gently pushes me toward a wood and clothe screen, "Try these on for now. If none of them fit, leave them on that table and come find me."

I watch Martha go to a different room where I hear her humming and rummaging through some more stuff. I go behind the screen and try the clothes on. To my surprise, they fit me perfectly. How does she do that? I then put my black and blue dress back on along with my black boots.

Levi Taylor

Then I take the clothes in my arms and go search for Martha.

I find Martha rummaging through some things in a cedar trunk. She looks up at me, than she takes me to a different room with even more shelves of stuff. "I'd like you to go through the blankets and curtains on the far wall. Anything you find that you like, take it. Then on the opposite of that are some towels and robes for when you go to the bathhouse. Take a few things from there and put all of your stuff on the table with the rest of your clothes. I'll put everything in a basket for you. Then we can wait for Nasir."

So I go through the blankets and chose a few that were green with a gold flower design as a border, and another that was a light green. I pick some green curtains that match the blanket with the gold design on it to. I pick a green and gold robe for the bathhouse, and a few dark green towels.

I take this stuff out to Martha in the front room. From there Martha puts that stuff in a basket with the rest of my clothes. I sit in a chair by the fireplace and watch the flames dance to their own song that we could not hear. Martha then sits down in a different chair and starts sewing.

Chapter Two
Ena

An hour later, Martha gets up and answers the door. She lets in a man who appears to be in his mid forties. His bleached blond hair was pulled back in a very neat ponytail. Martha introduces him, "Ena dear, this is Nasir. He'll be taking you to your new home. Nasir will also be teaching you how to work with the animals."

I thank Martha and follow Nasir who speaks to me in a stern voice, "As you heard before, I am Nasir. My oldest son, Ashi helps me out with the animals quite a bit. But lately he has been in bed sick. Until he is better, you will be taking his place. When he is better, I will assign you different work. I also took the liberty of taking your stuff from your horse up to your room. I gave your stallion a stall and feed."

We enter a big building. "Thank you Nasir."

"Do not thank me. Before lunch, I will show you how to tend to your horse and two other horses properly." Nasir takes me up a flight of stairs and opens a door at the end of the hallway, "This will be your room. There is not much, so do what you please with it."

Nasir leaves me alone in my new room. Looking around, I see a desk and bed by the only window. In between the desk and door was a well-built shelving unit. At the end of the bed was a dresser made out of cherry wood then stained. In one corner was a screen made out of cherry wood with a table and little stool, which was covered with royal green silk. All the wood furniture was made from cherry wood and stained. Sighing, I begin to unpack everything of mine.

After unpacking, I change into some different clothes. I put a pair of black pants on with a dark blue long sleeve shirt. I switch my expensive boots for a pair of old worn black boots. I then brush my hair out and put it back up in a much neater braid than before.

I just put my brush down when someone knocked on my door. Soon after the knock, the door opens and a boy around the age of sixteen comes in. He looked exactly like Nasir except for the green eyes and the age difference thing. He also looked to be at the height of five foot four inches maybe even slightly taller than that.

"Excuse me for intruding, but I am Rysin. My father, Nasir requests you down at the stables. If you are ready, I can take you to him."

I nod my head and follow Rysin. Down the stairs and to the stables we went. When we arrived at the stables, Nasir was waiting patiently on a crate. The boy leaves and Nasir gets up, "Let's hurry up. Lunch is in less than an hour."

I follow the man inside. He shows me how to groom horses. Then he sets me up with three horses, one of them being mine. At first the horses that did not belong to me were upset with a stranger touching them. After I soothed them, I was able to groom them along with my horse. After what seemed like forever was only maybe an hour.

I was just putting the brushes away when the blond boy, Rysin comes in. He informs me, "My father says it is time to eat. If you will follow me, I will show you where to wash up. From there we may head back and eat."

I finish putting everything away, and then I follow the boy to a well nearby. "How is it that a southerner, like you, raised in the middle of nowhere, has such good manners? It makes no sense."

I start to wash my hands while Rysin looks at my dumfounded and asks, "What?"

"Forgive me." I apologized, "That was rude of me. If I insulted you on accident, I am truly sorry. I did not mean for it to be an insult."

"No." interrupts Rysin, "It was not an insult. I am just surprised you asked."

This is quite surprising. Usually I get yelled at by now for asking such questions. How weird. These southerners are beginning to confuse me more than I need to be.

"It's just, I have never met any southerners who have been so kind and have such nice manners. All the southerners I have met were quite cruel and took everything I said as an insult. Then others were quiet and not really friendly."

The boy looks at me with his forest green eyes for sometime before breaking out laughing. "You really are a northerner! Amazing! You northerners have no clue what a real southerner is. The people you are describing live somewhere in between the north and south. They don't count as southerners or northerners." He takes a deep breath before asking, "What about you Ena? How is it you have better manners than most of the real northerners that we meet passing through?"

We head toward the house. "My family is very rich. I guess you can call us a very noble family. I was raised with good manners. If I spoke out of line, I was punished. For the punishment, my mother would wash ours, mostly my mouth, out with soap. Then at the age of twelve, my mother put me in the best school. Mostly she did it so I may learn discipline. At the school, the punishment for speaking out of term was to be locked up in a pitch-black room. I still think it was a broom closet at one point. Back to what I was saying, they would lock you up for two days in the room with no food or water. It was very scary, but it never taught me a thing."

"That's terrible. Washing someone's mouth out with soap is one thing, but locking them up is the worst, especially if they didn't give you food or water. It's just terrible."

Inside the house, I take my dirty boots off and follow Rysin down the hall into the kitchen. The smell of garlic and chicken filled the air. Then there was the freshly baked loaf of bread. Nasir was just getting table set.

At the table, I noticed a boy about the same age as Rysin.

But he had Nasir's midnight blue eyes. He had thick black hair pulled back in a messy ponytail. And his skin, it was so pale. He must be ill.

When the boy spoke, his voice sounded very weak. As though it was raw from coughing a lot. Poor fellow. "Who is the girl Rysin? Your girlfriend?"

"Ashi, enough! There is no reason for you to be acting like this." Snaps Nasir, "Ena here will be living with us. Mistress Raven has asked us to let her stay here and to welcome her as though she is part of the family. Also she has to work for me. So when you are finally feeling well again, I will give her some work in the barn to do."

Rysin leans toward to me and whispers, "Did I forget to mention, some of us southerners choose to use our manners? Only a few of us."

Then I whisper back, "Yes you did. And thank you for telling me so late."

Ashi looks at me. Then he asks, "Where are you from girl?"

Girl! Girl! For his information, I have a name. And it is not Girl. It is Ena. Men these days, calling us young ladies Girl just because they don't know our name. It disgusts me.

I answer his question very kindly, "I am from the far north. To be precise, I am from a city called Sira."

That is when Ashi looked at me weird. "A well educated one to be precise. Why don't you just go home where you belong? No one wants you here."

Staying calm, I reply, "Oh really? You are making it sound like you want me here."

Ashi snapped and stood up. His blanket fell off his shoulders, "You stupid northerner! Just leave already! And go home! You are not wanted here!"

At this point Nasir was getting pretty upset himself, "Ashi, that is…"

I interrupt Nasir, "Excuse me Nasir, but allow me." I turn my attention back to Ashi, "Thank you for the complement Ashi. And for your information, I am never going home unless someone puts a spell on me and drags me home. I may be a northerner, but I am not easily offended by words or really anything. Call me whatever you wish, but that will not scare me off. My northerner accent and I will be staying and I will work till my body cannot take any more. May we eat now?"

The three men just look at me dumbfounded. Have they never met a girl who could not be hurt by words? Or is it that they never met a well-dedicated northerner who speaks her mind? Whatever it is, these southerners will know not to try and chase me off like this again.

Nasir puts the rest of the food on the table, "If you two are done arguing, it is time to eat."

We sit down around the table and have a good meal. Everything tasted delicious. Half way through our meal, Ashi started coughing terribly.

Nasir gets up and helps his son Ashi to his feet, "When you two are done eating, clean up. Then I want Ena at the stables."

From there Nasir disappears with Ashi up the creaky old steps.

"This is going to take forever to clean up." Complains Rysin.

I get up and fold Ashi's blanket up leaving it on a table in the hallway. "I have a special soap that can help us clean the dishes faster and also make washing dishes very fun. What do you say?" I offered.

Rysin just grins, "Go get it. The faster we get done, the faster you can help my father."

So, I run up the creaky steps, and to my room. I open a small wood box and choose two small but different containers. I close the box and head back downstairs. I show Rysin a blue straight container, then a purple curvy container.

"The blue one is supposed to smell like the ocean." I explain, "And the purple one is lavender scented. Which one do you want to use?"

Rysin studies the containers then carefully picks up the blue one, "Let's go with the ocean scented one."

Nasir

It has been almost an hour. Where is that girl? And how long could cleaning up take?

Then all of a sudden, I see a girl with red hair running my way. She stops in front of me and catches her breath. "Forgive me for being late Nasir. I did not mean to keep you waiting. I like Rysin and I took advantage of cleaning up. We took the liberty, and washed all the dirty dishes for you."

'That must explain why the sleeves of your shirt are soaked. Do not worry about me scolding you for being late. You did me a big favor. I will not scold you as long as you tell me why you are late. I will scold you if you tell me a lie. Is that clear Ena?"

She replies, "Yes sir. And I also hope you do not mind your dishes smelling like the ocean breathe."

Sighing I ask, "Did you happen to use magic?"

Ena stares at me like I am stupid. Then she asks, "Why in the world would you think that? It is a scented soap we used. Yes I used magic to make the soap awhile back. But I did not use magic to help wash the dishes."

"I see. As long as you did not use magic. Now help me finish tending to these horses here. Or I will have to send you back to Mistress Raven."

She gets the supplies out and begins grooming a horse. We were brushing the horses for almost twenty minutes in silence when Ena asks, "Why does everyone call Raven Mistress Raven? Why not call her Head master or something more formal like Lady Raven. To me, mistress is just too much, unless you are married and have a child or two. Then again that is my definition of Mistress."

I had to laugh. When I began laughing, this caused Ena to stop and look at me, "What is so funny?"

I explain to Ena, "Mistress Raven is a Mistress. She is married. And she has one child at this point."

The girl looks at me dumbfounded and embarrassed. She soon busies herself with the horses.

"Mistress Raven is married to our healer Kirthis. She has an immortal child who is about your age. But she is never around. Mistress Raven's daughter's name is Kloe. Kloe loves to travel. Rarely does she come home."

Again Ena asks some more questions, "Why doesn't she come home? Doesn't she want to see her parents?"

"Kloe, she does not get along with her parents. She is stubborn and will not listen to them. Now let's finish with these horses. I have other things to do."

• • •
Ena

I help Nasir finish grooming the horses. After I was done, I go wash up. As I was on my way to the house, Martha finds me.

"Ena dear, has anyone shown you around yet?" asks Martha.

I shake my head, "No ma'am. Would you be kind enough to show me around? I do not need to get myself lost running an errand or something for someone."

Martha smiles gently, "Come along then dear. I'll show you around and maybe even introduce you to some of the other adults who work here."

After Martha shows me around and introduces me to almost all the adults who work here, she walks me home. I go up the creaky stairs and to my room at the end of the hallway. First thing I did when I entered my room was to have a sneezing attack.

Ugh! Dust! I go back downstairs and outside to the well. I get a bucket of water and carry it back up to my room. Then I pick everything up off the floor.

Ok, this is maybe the only time I may break the rules. I summon up a gust of wind and send it through my room to collect as much dust as it could. Then I got started.

I take some soap, from a green container, into the water. The aroma filled my nostrils' with the smell of the forest after a shower.

Then I get on my hands and knees and start scrubbing the floor. When I was done, I dumped the water outside. On my way upstairs, I think someone was telling me supper was done, but I was too tired and ignored them. I kick my boots off and collapse on my bed. I was out before my head hit the pillows.

Levi Taylor

. . .
Ligus

"Ena? Ena Scanrall? Where have I heard that name before? Or why does Scanrall ring a bell?"

I read over the note my dear friend Raven sent me:

'Dear Ligus, I need you to keep an eye on a girl for me. Her name is Ena Scanrall. She is working for me under Nasir's eyes, but I need your help. She is a magician. I need you to watch her and make sure she doesn't use any magic to get through her chores faster.'

"Magic? That's it!" I know there is a family who go by Scanrall living in the far north. Only one of their children can perform magic. And that child went to the Northern Lights Academy, the best in the country for magicians. This must be whom Raven is talking about. But there is no such person called Ena Scanrall. Perhaps this girl changed

The Lost Religion

her name to Ena but kept her last name for a good cause. I would like to know why.

I walk to my desk and open a drawer. I pull a piece of parchment out and a new quill pen. Then I sit down and respond back:

'My dear friend Raven,

I am willing to keep an eye on this girl called Ena Scanrall for you. I will come into the Narlin village near by tomorrow morning. I will be staying for some time or as long as you need me to stay. As a test, I would like to have the girl come looking for me. Describe what I look like to the girl, and send her into the village with someone who needs to run some errands. I will see how long it takes for her to find me, till then. I almost forgot! I will be wearing the traditional blue robes like always.

Ligus.'

I tie this piece of parchment to Raven's hawk's leg. Then I send it off. I am looking forward to meeting one of the Lord Scanrall's children.

Chapter Three
Ena

"Ena. Ena. You need to get up."

Opening my eyes, I find the early bird Nasir standing over me. He walks over to my window and opens it to let the light from the sun in.

I sit up rubbing my eyes. The blankets fall forward. Did someone cover me up while I slept? Who cares?

"I need you to go up town with Rysin today. Hurry up and get dressed now. He will be waiting at the stables for you." From there, Nasir leaves my room.

I was tempted to crawl back under my covers, but what was the use when the sun was out. I get up and choose some clothing. Feeling tired I decide to go with the same colors I wore yesterday; a nicer dark blue long sleeve top and a nice pair of black dress pants. After I was dressed, I put my hair back up in a ponytail. This is starting to become a hassle. I'll need to cut it in a week or two.

I was sitting on my bed lacing up my boots when I looked out the window. I noticed how dull the sun was shining, but there wasn't a cloud in sight. How can that be? It makes no sense at all.

I jump, no more like bounce off my bed. I grab my pouch of money and tie it around my waist. I go to my door and open to find the Black Raven standing there dressed in all black again.

All of a sudden I feel like I am back at the academy.

"You are tagging along with Rysin to town? I need you to do me a favor. I need you to find an elf that goes by the name Ligus. He has blond long hair and blue eyes. He will be wearing the traditional blue robes of his hometown. Will you be capable of finding Ligus?"

Levi Taylor

I nod my head not wanting to anger the Black Raven in any way. She was already frightening by the way she dressed. As the Black Raven gracefully walks down the hallway, her cloak swims ever so slightly behind her.

I run downstairs almost running into the wall. I hurry outside and run to the stables. When I reached the stables, Rysin had just finished saddling his and my horse. How nice of him.

We get on the horses, me on my beautiful chocolate stallion, and Rysin on his gray mustang. From there we head east. While we rode, I tried to absorb everything about this beautiful land.

The river was crystal clear with fish playing peek a boo. The trees were swaying ever so slightly in the gentle breeze. And the flowers! There were so many of them in so many beautiful colors. There were clearings, which held all sorts of blossoming flowers. The smell was wonderful. It was so calm and peaceful. I didn't want leave.

"Rysin, who is this elf called Ligus? Mistress Raven has asked me to find him. Can you help me please?"

"I'm sorry, but I cannot help. Mistress Raven told me not to help you. I can say, it will be hard since you have never met him. Just do your best." Says Rysin.

"Boy wasn't that helpful. Maybe I should go ask a cow or even better, a donkey."

Rysin bursts out laughing, "You need to learn to find people when someone describes who you're looking for. Especially now that you will be working for Mistress Raven."

Getting irritated I ask, "Fine! But how is it everything I happen to say is funny to everyone else? I'm not very fond of people laughing at me. Is it what I say or how I say it? I would really like to know."

Rysin starts laughing less, "It is both. The way you speak

and say it is quite funny especially with that northerner accent of yours. Your accent and tone of your voice you speak in is what makes me laugh."

Was he drunk or something? Having had enough, I go over to Rysin and push him off his horse. I grab the reins of his horse as well as mine and start riding away at a steady gallop. Over my shoulder I yell, "That was for insulting me. You'll have to walk the rest of the way."

Then I encourage the horses to a slightly faster speed. When the town got closer, I got off my horse and lead the two horses into town. How in the world am I supposed to find this Ligus? I look for almost an hour, when I finally decided to use my gift.

My gift allows me to see everyone's aura. I close my eyes and slowly open them. To everyone else, my eyes would appear purple while I am using my gift. When I am done, they will go back to their ocean blue. I look at everyone's aura. Most of the auras were blue representing the mortal humans. Now and then there would be a splash of purple for the immortals in town. Just as I was ready to give up, I saw a flash of white from the corner of my eye. I turn toward it to see a single figure with white aura coming from them.

I return to my normal vision. In front of me a few yards stood a very handsome elf. He had such light blond hair; you would think it was the sun. His eyes were as blue as a glass orb; shimmering when light bounced off it. The elf was very tall, and slender. He had flawless skin just like my father.

I finally get the courage and walk over to the elf. Once I get to the elf, I stop and state, "Excuse me, but I have been instructed to find you; orders from Mistress Raven. Just to be sure, would you be kind enough to tell me your name Sir."

"I am Ligus. And who are you young lady?"

Finally, some respect! Out of nowhere runs a blond boy. Took him long enough to get here. Rysin comes running over and yells, "Ena! Why in the world did you leave me behind?"

I question him, "Did you not hear me when I left you on your own? Do not insult me. Just because others don't get offended easily does not mean I wont. It is very easy to offend me. Now here is your horse." I said handing him the reins to his horse.

. . .
Ligus

This girl in front of me was Ena? How's it her father is an elf and she is not? She does have our flawless skin, but in a much paler tone than it should be. Her height is nowhere that it should be for an elf.

I watch as Rysin and this Ena argue about something.

Finally I ask, "Are you Ena Scanrall, the same Scanrall who attended the Northern Light Academy for magicians?"

Rysin just stares at Ena, who is staring at me with such icy eyes. Rysin finds the courage to ask, "You're a magician?"

Ena replies grumpily, "Yes. And I have been a magician for a decade and a half. I am Ena Scanrall. I am the Scanrall who attended the academy you speak of. Why do you ask such questions Sir?"

Levi Taylor

I'm getting the impression that she does not want to speak of the academy, that and she acts as if she has a grudge against elves or something.

I decide to tell her, "My friend Raven has asked me come to keep an eye on you dear Ena."

She just asks, "Why? Am I not capable of taking care of myself?"

"I was asked by Raven, to make sure you do not use magic when doing your chores. Raven would keep an eye on you herself, but as you may know, she is a very busy woman."

"Like I asked before, am I not capable of taking care of myself? And rarely do I use magic. I only use magic for protection. I have weapons to fight with."

She definitely has a problem with elves or maybe it's just me. Either way, I don't like it. "Rysin, go ahead and do your shopping. When you are done, head back home. Tell Raven that Ena will be helping me with my shopping.

Rysin nods his head and takes his horse from Ena, "Yes Sir. I understand."

I watch as he gets going on his horse. When he was out of sight, I turn to Ena and demand, "What is your problem? I don't know why you hate me or elves so much, but it needs to stop!"

She gives me a look, "Forgive my manners, but you are an idiot. I do not dislike you or elves unless it has to do with my family. I did not appreciate that you brought up the academy. I have a lot of bad memories from there. Another reason I am in a grumpy mood is, I did not eat dinner last night or eat breakfast this morning. Then to top it off, Rysin offended me on our way here. So I am very grumpy."

She is a true Scanrall all right. Grumpy when she had not

eaten. And she is even grumpier when someone offends her when she was already grumpy. I offer, "Why don't we go grab something to eat. Then we can talk. I'll even pay for the food. Does that sound good dear Ena?"

Ena just says, "Lead the way."

Ena

I follow this elf to a place to eat. We tie our horses up and go inside. Ligus leads me to a table. We take our seats and order something to eat.

"Tell me, how is it your father is an elf and you are not? It doesn't make any sense to me."

I really wish he would stop bringing up my past and personal issues, "I will only, and only answer this question. If you are wondering why I do not wish to answer your questions, it's because I don't like people snooping through my past or personal issues."

Ligus takes a sip of his tea, "I understand, but I'm still waiting for you to answer my question."

This elf is starting to get on my nerves, "My father and his second wife are elves. My father's first wife, my real mother, was an immortal. I had a twin but he passed away when we were only ten. He passed away from an illness no one could cure. My brother looked more like an elf than I ever will. He looked more like our father while I look more like our real mother. So I guess you can say I am half elf, and half immortal. I hope you're happy now."

Ligus again sips his tea, "I understand now. I have heard rumors, but never believed them. I think now I do believe in those rumors."

I take a sip of my tea and add, "Also I forgot to mention this. I prefer to call myself an immortal instead of an elf. If I tell people I'm an elf; they'll just deny it. Plus I get tired of having to explain what I just explained to you."

We stopped talking when our food arrived. After we finished our meal, I follow this elf throughout town. We end up in an old looking store. Everything in the store was ancient or just plain old. Ligus went in one direction of the store, while I decided to look at some books.

A few minutes later, Ligus calls for me, "Ena, could you come over here for a minute."

I leave the books and walk over to him to find him going through some very old but beautiful clothes. "Do you think these would fit you in anyway?"

I reply after looking at them for a few seconds, "Maybe. Why do you ask?"

He doesn't answer me, but only goes up to the front and purchases them along with several books.

After shopping all day, we get on our horses and hit the road. The ride home was quiet, too quiet. For some reason, the ride back wasn't peaceful. There was this sinister feeling lingering in the air. It was to the point where it began causing me to shiver.

Ligus notices my shivering, "Ena, are you cold?"

Lying through my teeth, "No." Apparently my lie didn't work because Ligus guides his horse over to mine and drapes his cloak over my shoulders. Then he tells me in a nice cool gentle voice, "Keep the cloak. I have more where that came from."

From there, the rest of the trip back was boring and very quiet. When we reached the house, the wind had begun to pick up. I take the stuff Ligus bought for me up to my room, while Nasir shows Ligus his room. Rysin was taking care of our horses for us.

While putting my new clothes up, I stumble upon a small Old book and a beautiful statue.

I open the book to find it empty at first. Then like magic, words began appearing. After closing the book, the cover had a simple bird behind the title   "The Holy Bible." I have no clue what it is about or what 'Holy Bible' means. I guess I'll have to read it when I have time.

The statue was just marvelous. It was of a girl with wings. The girl had her eyes closed and head tilted upwards. The girl's hair was out behind her as though the wind was blowing through it. Her dress was long and beautiful and white. She was holding an orb of some sort in her palms. It was so magical, almost like it could be real.

I put the book and statue on my desk, and finish putting the clothes away. Then I head downstairs and join everyone for supper. Ashi was missing, so his illness must of got the best of him today.

Levi Taylor

• • •

Ligus

At dinner, I notice Ena has been shivering nonstop. Getting annoyed with it, I ask, "Ena, are you coming down with a cold? You've been shivering ever since we returned from uptown."

Ena just stares at me, "No. I've been cold all day. It's nothing."

Why does this girl keep lying to me? Sighing, I stand up and walk over to Ena. I place my hand on her forehead. She felt slightly colder than normal. "You are cold, but I guess you're not coming down with a cold. Nasir, can we add more wood to the main fire? We don't need Ena getting sick, or Ashi getting worst."

Nasir gets up and adds some more wood warming the house up. Both Nasir and I return to our seat. Rysin then asks, "Ena, how can you be so cold? You're always wearing a long sleeve shirt."

The Lost Religion

Ena just shrugs and returns to her food. Then Nasir asks, "During the day you should be wearing a shorter sleeve shirt, instead of a long sleeve shirt. I really don't need you to pass out from the heat while working."

Poor Ena stares at them for some time. Then she rises slowly and says, "Excuse me, but I'm no longer hungry." She walks away.

To Nasir and Rysin, I say, "That was very rude. Both of you should know better."

Chapter Four
Ena

Not wanting to answer Rysin or his father, I stand up and excuse myself. From there, I walk upstairs to my room. Once in my bedroom, I pull the book I found earlier out and open it. The first page had a content. The content was divided into two parts. Books of the Old Testament, and Books of the New Testament. There were thirty-one names under the Old Testament, and twenty-seven names under the New Testament. Maybe these names were books within books. I guess I'll have to read.

Turning the page, I began to read: *"In the beginning God created the heaven and the earth."*

Who is this God? Is heaven where the dead go? And what is earth? To myself I say, "Great, now I'm all confused." So instead of being confused, I continue to read:

"And the earth was without form, and void; and darkness was upon the face of the deep. And the Spirit of God moved upon the face of the waters. And God said, 'Let there be light': and there was light. And God saw the light, that it was good: and God divided the light from the darkness."

Grabbing my empty journal and something to write with, I begin to rewrite each line. Beside each line, I write my thoughts about it down.

'The light is referring to the day; and the darkness refurring to the night. How strange, that this God could do all of this in so little time.' I thought, 'Amazing.'

As I kept reading, I learned this God made the water, the earth, and all living beings. The first living human was called Adam. He named all the animals. Even then, being the only human he was still lonely. So God put Adam in a deep sleep. From there God took one of Adam's ribs and created Eve, Adams female lover.

Levi Taylor

. . .

Ligus

After helping Nasir clean up, I go up to my room. There I sit in bed and read one of my books. It was maybe an hour or so after reading, I got thirsty. So putting my book aside, I get up and go downstairs. I get something to drink. It was on my way back to my room that I realize there was a light on in Ena's room.

I knock on the door lightly, "Ena, are you still up?"

When no one replied, I open the door. I find Ena asleep at her desk. Her beautiful maroon hair was down. She looked so peaceful.

I walk over to her and gently shake her awake. She sits up half asleep rubbing her eyes, "What do you want Ligus?"

I tell her, "It's getting late. You need to go to bed if you're to help Nasir tomorrow."

The Lost Religion

I watch her as she puts a book and journal away. Then she goes over to her bed and crawls in bed. As soon as her head hit the pillow, I knew she was out cold. I go over to her and cover her up with some blankets. Then I blow the candles out.

I close her door as I leave, then I head down the hall to my room. I decide to go to bed. I lay my book on the desk and go to bed myself.

Levi Taylor

. . .

Ena

I wake up under some blankets. When I try to get up, I got tangled up in my blankets. Instead of standing, I fall out of bed, with a loud thud. I know someone heard me because my door opens. When I got myself untangled, I look up to see Ligus standing above me.

"Ena are you alright?" Asks Ligus.

"Am I all right? Is that it!" For some reason I yell at Ligus, "Ligus! Do I look all right to you? I just fell out of bed from being tangled up in my blankets. Who in the world covered me up?"

Ligus sighs, "That would be me. I covered you up. None of this would have happened if you had gone to bed. Instead you stayed up reading. Next time, go to bed on time and won't have to accidentally fall out of bed."

I was just about to argue back when Nasir comes in asking, "What is all the commotion about? Some of us would like very much to sleep."

Before I could even open my mouth, Ligus says, "Ena fell out of bed and is yelling at me. She decided to blame me."

Nasir says, "Well enough of this yelling. I don't care if you two are arguing, but do when everyone's up. Go back to bed both of you."

Nasir leaves the room leaving me with Ligus.

Ligus says, "Well, I'm going back to bed. I hope you are too."

From there Ligus leaves my room. I go and slam my door shut. Being fed up, I change into some clean clothes. When I was dressed, my hair was brushed and put up. I then go outside. I run across the road to the practice arena for magicians. I put up a barrier so no magic would leak

67

Levi Taylor

out. Once that task was done, I begin to practice some magic.

As soon as I was finished, I look up to see a pale Ashi watching me. Ashi looked almost like a ghost. I let my barrier evaporate into thin air. I walk over to the pale boy and ask, "Shouldn't you be in bed resting?"

Ashi looks at me with this distant stare. Apparently the cold wasn't affecting him, but it sure was giving me goose bumps. Ashi slowly walks over to me, "You're a magician correct?"

"Yes I am. Why are you asking? Is there something you want me to do for you?" I was trying to be nice since he's been sick for some time. Maybe he wants me to do a little performance to lift his mood.

Ashi comes closer, "I am ill if you cannot tell. I have been ill for over a month. My life has been taken over by it. I would like it back please." He coughs into his hand. His coughing got the better of him forcing him to his knees. When he was done coughing, I help him up. He continues, "I would like it if you could heal me. Please, I'm begging you. I want my life back."

All I could do was stare. No one has ever asked such a thing from me. What was I suppose to do. I am no healer, and I don't know how to heal anyone. "Ashi." I say gently, "I am no healer. I don't know how. I was taught to use my magic for fighting. If I knew how to heal, I would help. I am sorry, but I think I can help you in a way."

"What is that?" asks Ashi. I take a deep breath, "My mother taught me how to make medicine for the ill. I could make some medicine that can help you in some possible way. But I'm not sure it will work."
Ashi questions me, "If you can make medicine, doesn't that make you a healer?"

"You have a good point. Anyway, if you hold still, I can send my magic through you to find out what is causing you to be ill. Then I can work on your medicine from there. Is that ok?" The ill boy wasn't sure, but he nodded his head in agreement. He holds still while I put a hand on his shoulder. I close my eyes and send my magic flowing through his blood stream looking for the cause of his illness. I definitely could sense something wrong, but I couldn't put my tongue on it.

My eyes flash open as I feel something sharp pierce my skin. All I could see was this dull red aura and blackness. What is happening, God! Help me. Do not let my life end here! Please help me! From there the darkness consumed me.

• • •
Lingus

Sitting up in bed, sweat rolls down my face. My breath was short and quick. I stand up and use the bed frame to support me. I was dizzy. I let my breathe even out. Soon I stopped sweating.

For a minute I thought I heard Ena. Maybe she just fell out of bed again. It is possible. But for some reason, I feel as thou she is in danger. Not sure what was really going on, I run down to Ena's room. Empty? Where could she be? I don't get it. How could she not be in her room? Maybe she wanted something to drink.

I make my way to the kitchen. There was a light on. Nasir looks up from the table and asks, "Where is Ashi? He's not in his room resting like he should be. I can't find him."

"Ena isn't in her room either. I have a terrible feeling that she is in danger. I need to find her now."

Both Nasir and I check the house again. We then go outside and stop in our track. Not far away, Ashi was standing over an unconscious Ena. She wasn't moving, but there was blood from some sort of wound.

I run over to Ena while Nasir runs to his son. Ashi looked at us with sorrow in his eyes. Through tears, the boy apologizes, "I am so sorry. I didn't mean to. She was trying to help. I am so sorry. Please forgive me. I tried to stop, but I couldn't. Please, oh please forgive me."

Nasir leads his son away assuring him it was all right. I rip my robe up some and put it on Ena's neck wound. Holding that there, I clean her blood stream of any venom that might be lurking there.

Not far, I hear the father tell his son to take some type of antidote. I gently pick the young immortal girl up. I take her inside to her room where I carefully lay her on the bed.

Nasir already took Ashi to his room. Then soon left to fetch the healer Kirthis. I waited for maybe only a few minutes for Kirthis.

A man with brunette hair and hazel eyes comes in. He comes over to where Ena was and begins tending to her wounds. I watch Ena hoping, more like praying that whatever gods are listening; they will spare the girl's life.

When Kirthis was done, he looks at me, "Sir Ligus, do not worry. Miss Scanrall will be fine. A few days in bed and a few days of taking it easy, she'll be her normal busy self."

He leaves before I could ask him any questions. I take a seat at Ena's desk. Looking around, I notice a statue. It was of a girl with wings. Before I could inspect the statue, Martha comes in. She looks at Ena then me. Shaking her head she says to me, "Dear, you need to change your clothes and go back to sleep. While you are sleeping, I will watch over Ena for you. When you get up, you may watch over her."

Levi Taylor

I get up and head down the where my room is. I change out of my stained clothes and go to bed. Lying in bed, I close my eyes and take a deep breathe hoping that she will be ok.

Chapter Five
Nasir

In the morning, Ligus comes downstairs dressed. I had just finished cleaning up. "You look disturbed Ligus. What is it?"

The man takes a seat and looks at me, "Nasir, how long have you known that Ashi had been transforming into a vampire?"

Taking a seat across of the elf, I rest my head in my hands, "I've known for some time now. Kirthis made an antidote for him. The healer told me not to give it to Ashi unless he went for blood. And I'm very sorry that Ena was the victim."

Ligus stares at me upset. "You're sorry? How can you just sit there calmly and tell me that you're sorry! Ena could have been killed. What if she had been killed, then what?

What would I say to her father?"

"Ligus, there is no need to yell. Ena is alive and well. You can speak to her later when she is up. Just calm down please. Ena and Ashi are still asleep."

"I want to know, why did you wait this long? Why didn't you give Ashi the antidote sooner? It would have stopped the transforming before he got to the blood thirsty part."

Sighing, I ask, "Why do you care so much about Ena? She is an immortal you have just met. You know nothing about her. And even I don't know anything about her past. What does Ena mean to you?"

Amazing, the elf shuts up and looks surprised. "Is it alright for a elf my age to fall in love with a immortal girl?"

So that is why he cares so much about her. "It is possible. Now thinking of it, I think it's quite noticeable. When you arrived here from town with Ena, I could tell then. The

The Lost Religion

way you looked and still look at her is the same look that I gave when I first met my wife. But there is nothing wrong with you falling in love with Ena."

"I never believed in the phrase, 'Love at first sight'. Now I do. What am I going to do? What if she doesn't love me? What do I do?" Ligus puts his head down on the table.

Leaning in on the table toward the man, "I can't tell you if the girl loves you or not. She hides her feelings from everyone all the time. Her temper is probably the only emotion she will show along with her seriousness."

Ligus looks up at me; "There is something about Ena that makes her mysterious. She's not an open book alright, but you can tell there are a lot of things she does not want to talk about."

"That's where you come in. Ena needs someone to help her through whatever it is she's going through. Her secrets need to be exposed. Then she can get help. She

Levi Taylor

tries to forget about her past, but when someone brings something up, it just about makes her want to cry."

More to himself, the elf says, "Maybe that's why she avoids almost all of my questions."

Ena

Waking up in my room was confusing. First I was outside, and now I'm in my room. As I tried to sit up, someone gently pushes me down on my shoulders. I look to my right to see a blond elf. Not just any elf, Sir Ligus the elf.

My head began to hurt for some reason, and I was hungry. Almost like someone read my mind, Nasir comes in. He puts a tray of food on the desk, and then comes over to me. The man helps me sit up and says, "I see you finally decided to wake up. Tell me, how are you feeling right now?"

"I'm tired and hungry. And right now, I have a headache." Ligus chuckles at me. I look at him, "What is so funny?"

Ligus sits on the windowsill, "What's funny is you. Of course you're going to be hungry and tired. You were attacked by a vampire."

Levi Taylor

"A what?" ask I.

Ligus went to explain, but Nasir interrupts, "Ligus, now isn't the time. You can tell her after she gets some food in her and rests some more. Just don't say a word about it till then. And as for you Ena, you don't have to worry about it. Just focus on getting better."

I guess it's not that important. Plus, I forgot about it as soon as Nasir places the food in font of me. I realize how hungry I really was. My stomach was grumbling. The smell of garlic, with a hint of sage, along with that the smell of chicken was so mouth watering. And it tasted just as good as it smelled. The tea was cinnamon and apple.

I haven't had anything like this in a long time. My dry throat was soothed with the tea. All this hot food made me feel better and chases my headache away.

When I finished eating, Nasir takes the empty dishes away. Someone helps me lay back down. I close my eyes and let myself drift to sleep where all my dreams awaited me.

The healer Kirthis had me, more like demanded that I stay in bed for a few days. Either way, I slept those days. When I was finally aloud out of bed, Nasir refused to give me any type of work. Instead, I am stuck in the house with the elf Ligus. What fun.

While the elf reads, I pace around the house looking for stuff to do. Unable to find anything to keep me busy, I go down to the kitchen. There, I sit across of Ligus at the kitchen table.

Ligus looks up from his reading, "Can't find anything to occupy yourself?"

I complain, "I'm bored. Nasir won't let me help out in the stables. Neither of you will tell me what happened. And I can't find anything to do. I swear Nasir keeps this house spotless."

Levi Taylor

Sighing the elf puts down his book and looks at me with sad eyes, "Are you sure you really want to know?"

I prop my head on my hand and ask, "Why do you look so sad? And why are you making it a big deal?"

This elf man takes a deep breathe, "Ena, you were attacked. You could have died."

. . .
Ligus

She looks at me and gently laughs. Then returning her full attention to me, she asks, "Why does that matter? It seems like I'm always getting my self in life threatening positions. I'm used to it."

I ask her politely, "You really don't care if you die do you?"

And just like that she goes all serious on me. I could tell she was tensing up, "I do care now. Before I would have let a simple bandit take my life away. Now I have reasons to live. And because of those reasons, I am finding my place in life."

Ena slowly stands up and gives me a warm smile. This smile made my heart race and maybe skip a beat. I could feel my face burning. She leaves the kitchen and walks up the creaky stairs.

Levi Taylor

. . .

Ena

Leaving Ligus in the kitchen, I go up to my room. Once in my room, I close the door and flop down on the bed.

I close my eyes and begin drifting. I was almost asleep when the air started feeling heavy and cold like the one day.

It filled the space in my room causing me to sit straight up in bed. I open my eyes and notice my window. It was open. I haven't opened it all day. Why was it open and who opened it?

I look around. The room was dark, weird since it was daylight outside. I couldn't see anyone, and no one came through the door or I would have heard them. Sighing I close my eyes and activate my Sight. I jump back surprised to see the blazing orange aura walking around. Slowly I get up out of bed.

. . .
Ligus

It's been some time now since Ena went upstairs. Maybe she decided to take a nap. I go back to my book just as a lot of magic was being used. It was coming from upstairs. I drop my book and run upstairs lightning fast only to run into someone or something.

· · ·

Ena

When I stood up, the aura of the person or thing stopped. It looks at me and a dull voice from it says, "You must die Ena Scanrall." The voice sounded like a male.

I was going to say something when this person threw me against the wall and held a dagger in his one hand. Knowing what he was planning to do with the dagger, I sent him flying through the window with a gust of wind. I open the door and run smack dab into Ligus.

Ligus demands worried, "Ena! What is going on?"

Hurrying downstairs, I say, "I'll tell you later!"

I rush outside to find the Black Raven sparring with this person. I race over to help, but the mysterious man jumps back onto a roof. He looks at me and says, "Do not think you got away Ena. The Dark Lord will send someone to finish what I could not." From there the man just disappeared into thin air. And I mean, he really just disappeared into thin air. It is so weird. A man, maybe a magician man, comes out of nowhere and attacks me. What makes it worse is I could not get a good look at his face. He was wearing all dark browns, and had an old dark red scarf covering up his face. That makes me so mad!

Then there is this Dark Lord. Who on earth is this Dark Lord? Those two words, Dark Lord, kept echoing in my head. Now I really have no clue what I have done to upset this Dark Lord.

Out of nowhere, Ligus interrupts my train of thoughts,

"Ena, what just happened? Why are your eyes purple?" Then he begins to freak, "One minute your eyes are blue, the next they are purple! What is going on?"

I take a few steps backwards away from Ligus. He was

freaking out and to be honest, he was scaring me. Usually elves don't freak out, but apparently this elf has a short fuse.

I look at the Black Raven. She was dumbfounded and staring at me. I return to my normal vision. The Black Raven asks me in a whisper, "You have the Sight?"

Ligus of course just freaks out some more, "The what? What in the world is this Sight? I have never heard of such a thing. Some tell me what is going on!"

Out of nowhere the Black Raven slaps the elf hard across the face. So hard across the face, that Ligus's head whips to the right and throws him to the ground. Now the Black Raven was yelling, "Get a hold of yourself! Ena has the Sight, which allows her to see all kinds of auras! If it wasn't for her Sight, she would be dead right now!"

The Black Raven turns around on her heels and walks like a queen away. I go over to Ligus and help him up.

He avoids looking at me and stares at the sky instead. "Thank you Ena. I do hope you will forgive me for the way I have just acted. It was uncalled for." apologizes Ligus.

"It's ok. I just know better not to anger you." I give him a friendly smile even if he was too embarrassed to look at me. "Do you know who this Dark Lord is?"

The elf's answer was too quick. "No I don't know. I have never heard of this Dark Lord."

I shrug my shoulders. "Oh well. I guess this Dark Lord is not that important. Your cheek is bleeding. Raven's nails must have given you a cut. Let me help." Before Ligus could get out of my reach, I had pulled a handkerchief out and gently pressed it against his cut. He winces gently. This causes him to look at me. I could tell by looking in his eyes, that he was in love with me.

Levi Taylor

"Keep the handkerchief. I can get another one later. You should go have Kirthis look at that. Then maybe later I can explain to you about my Sight. Sound like a plan?"

He answers, "Of course. And thank you again Ena."

"You can enter God's Kingdom only through the narrow gate. The highway to hell is broad, and its gate is wide for the many who choose the easy way. But the gateway to life is small, and the road is narrow, and only a few ever find it."

Matthew 7:13-14

Mrs. Bea's Publishing Company
P.O Box 424
Farmington, MI. 48332-0424

Owner and Founder
Author Terri F. Williams
Website
http//:www.authorterriwilliams.biz

Mrs. Bea's Kid's Publishing Company is proud to publish Author Levi Taylor's first book. Congratulations!!! Keep up the good work and keep writing!

Levi Taylor